Northern Mockingbirds

Julie Murray

Abdo Kids Junior
is an Imprint of Abdo Kids
abdobooks.com

Abdo
STATE BIRDS
Kids

abdobooks.com

Published by Abdo Kids, a division of ABDO, P.O. Box 398166, Minneapolis, Minnesota 55439. Copyright © 2022 by Abdo Consulting Group, Inc. International copyrights reserved in all countries. No part of this book may be reproduced in any form without written permission from the publisher. Abdo Kids Junior™ is a trademark and logo of Abdo Kids.

Printed in the United States of America, North Mankato, Minnesota.

052021

092021

Photo Credits: iStock, Minden Pictures, Shutterstock

Production Contributors: Teddy Borth, Jennie Forsberg, Grace Hansen

Design Contributors: Candice Keimig, Pakou Moua

Library of Congress Control Number: 2020947578

Publisher's Cataloging-in-Publication Data

Names: Murray, Julie, author.
Title: Northern mockingbirds / by Julie Murray
Description: Minneapolis, Minnesota : Abdo Kids, 2022 | Series: State birds | Includes online resources and index.
Identifiers: ISBN 9781098207175 (lib. bdg.) | ISBN 9781098208011 (ebook) | ISBN 9781098208431 (Read-to-Me ebook)
Subjects: LCSH: State birds--Juvenile literature. | Mockingbirds--Juvenile literature. | Birds--Behavior--United States--Juvenile literature.
Classification: DDC 598.297--dc23

Table of Contents

Northern Mockingbirds........4

State Bird..........22

Glossary...........23

Index..............24

Abdo Kids Code.....24

Northern Mockingbirds

Northern mockingbirds live in North America.

5

They live in open areas.

They are in backyards too!

They are gray in color.

Their bellies are white.

Their wings open when flying.

White patches appear.

They sing all day long. They copy sounds. Males can learn 200 songs!

They eat fruit and berries. They also eat worms and insects.

15

They build nests. Nests are made of twigs and grass.

Females lay 3 to 5 eggs.

The eggs are light blue.

They have brown spots.

The eggs **hatch** in 2 weeks.

Chicks can fly 12 days later.

State Bird

AR
Arkansas

FL
Florida

MS
Mississippi

TN
Tennessee

TX
Texas

Glossary

chick
a bird that has just hatched or a young bird.

hatch
to come out of an egg.

Index

chicks 20

color 8, 10, 18

eggs 18, 20

food 14

habitat 6

markings 10, 18

nest 16

North America 4

sounds 12

wings 10

Visit **abdokids.com** to access crafts, games, videos, and more!

Use Abdo Kids code **SNK7175** or scan this QR code!